Harry's Hat

A humorous story
in a familiar setting

First published in 2007 by
Franklin Watts
338 Euston Road
London
NW1 3BH

Franklin Watts Australia
Level 17 / 207 Kent Street
Sydney
NSW 2000

Text © Sue Graves 2007
Illustration © Belinda Worsley 2007

A CIP catalogue record for this book is available
from the British Library.

ISBN 978 0 7496 7132 7 (hbk)
ISBN 978 0 7496 7692 6 (pbk)

Series Editor: Jackie Hamley
Series Advisors: Dr Barrie Wade, Dr Hilary Minns
Design: Peter Scoulding

Printed in China

Franklin Watts is a division of
Hachette Children's Books.

The publisher would like to thank illustrator Hannah Turner
and Susan Clow at Scope's In the Picture project for their help
in the production of this book.

Visit www.childreninthepicture.org.uk
or www.scope.org.uk for more information.

Harry's Hat

Written by
Sue Graves

Illustrated by
Belinda Worsley

W
FRANKLIN WATTS
LONDON • SYDNEY

Sue Graves
"I love going to parties, don't you? My favourite parties are hat parties. They're the best ones of all!"

Belinda Worsley
"I live in Italy. It's very sunny in the summer, so I wear a big sun hat. But Harry's pirate hat is much more fun!"

It was Harry's birthday.

Happy Birthday

5

He got a hat.

6

Harry took it to school.

"Take that off, please!"
said Miss Lupin.

Harry went swimming.
He took his hat.

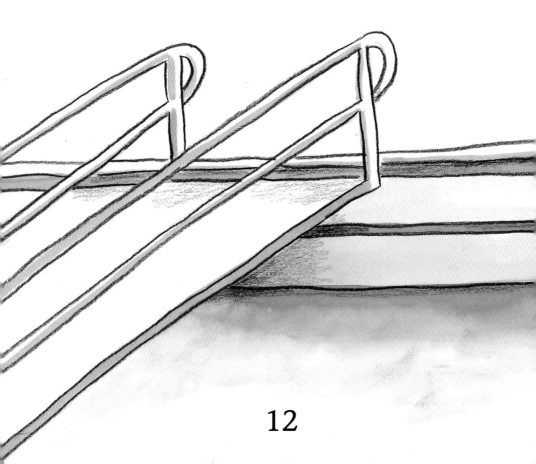

SWIMMING POOL

"Take that off, please!"
said Jim.

15

Harry was sad.

17

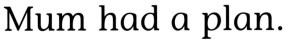

Mum had a plan.

18

Everyone came
to Harry's party.

Everyone had hats.
But Harry's was the
best hat of all!

23

Notes for parents and teachers

READING CORNER has been structured to provide maximum support for new readers. The stories may be used by adults for sharing with young children. Primarily, however, the stories are designed for newly independent readers, whether they are reading these books in bed at night, or in the reading corner at school or in the library.

Starting to read alone can be a daunting prospect. READING CORNER helps by providing visual support and repeating words and phrases, while making reading enjoyable. These books will develop confidence in the new reader, and encourage a love of reading that will last a lifetime!

If you are reading this book with a child, here are a few tips:

1. Talk about the story before you start reading. Look at the cover and the title. What might the story be about? Why might the child like it?

2. Encourage the child to reread the story, and to retell the story in their own words, using the illustrations to remind them what has happened.

3. Discuss the story and see if the child can relate it to their own experience, or perhaps compare it to another story they know.

4. Give praise! Small mistakes need not always be corrected.

READING CORNER covers three grades of early reading ability, with three levels at each grade. Each level has a certain number of words per story, indicated by the number of bars on the spine of the book, to allow you to choose the right book for a young reader:

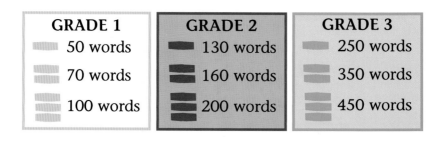

GRADE 1	GRADE 2	GRADE 3
50 words	130 words	250 words
70 words	160 words	350 words
100 words	200 words	450 words